ALICE and the BOA CONSTRICTOR

by Laurie Adams and Allison Coudert

ALICE and the BOA CONSTRICTOR

Illustrated by Emily Arnold McCully

Houghton Mifflin Company Boston 1983

Library of Congress Cataloging in Publication Data

Adams, Laurie.
  Alice and the boa constrictor.

  Summary: After learning in science class that boa
constrictors make wonderful pets, Alice saves her money
until she has enough to buy Sir Lancelot.
  [1. Boa constrictor—Fiction. 2. Snakes as pets—
Fiction] I. Coudert, Allison, 1941-   . II. McCully,
Emily Arnold, ill. III. Title.
PZ7.A21735Al 1983   [Fic]   82-15769
ISBN 0-395-33068-8

Printed in the United States of America

V 10 9 8 7 6 5 4 3 2 1

For Alexa, Caroline, and Polly

The authors gratefully acknowledge the inspiration
and assistance of Georgeanne Rousseau

Contents

1
Alice Has an Idea

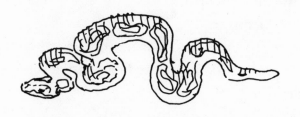

"**A** what?" spluttered Alice's father. His soup spoon clattered noisily against his soup bowl. The Whipple family had just sat down to their evening meal. Gerald Whipple worked in a bank on Wall Street and Mary Whipple taught reading for half a day while Alice and Beatrice were in school. Alice was in fourth grade and Beatrice was in kindergarten. Both attended Miss Barton's School for Girls. They took the school bus together every morning.

"A bo-a con-stric-tor, Daddy," Alice repeated, slowly separating the words into syllables as if her father had never heard of a boa constrictor. That was the way *he* pronounced the new spelling words she had to learn each week for her Friday spelling tests.

"I assume you are joking," Mr. Whipple replied in the dignified tone he reserved for serious situations.

Sometimes, Alice suspected, he used that tone when he was not sure what to say and was stalling for time.

"I don't think she is joking, dear," said Mrs. Whipple. "She is studying reptiles in Science." Mrs. Whipple collected the soup bowls and took them into the kitchen while Mr. Whipple began carving the roast.

"More milk, Mommy," called Beatrice.

"What's the magic word?"

"Oh, *please*, I suppose."

"Bring your glass in here," her mother called back.

"Could we please talk about my boa constrictor?" said Alice impatiently.

"It's not *your* boa constrictor," Beatrice said, sticking her tongue out when her father wasn't looking. "And if *she* gets one, then you have to get me something too." Beatrice sat down and blew bubbles into her milk.

"Who said anything about getting something — ouch!" Mr. Whipple's hand slipped on the roast and he cut his thumb. "Damn!" he shouted.

"You're not supposed to say bad words," Beatrice reminded him.

Mrs. Whipple rushed back from the kitchen. "Now what?" She set a platter of string beans in the center of the table.

"Yuck! I hate string beans." Beatrice pouted.

"Don't pout . . . baby, baby, baby," Alice said.

Beatrice started to cry.

"Oh for heaven's sake," Mr. Whipple groaned, shaking his thumb and then sucking it.

"Be careful, dear. Don't wave your hand around,"

said Mrs. Whipple calmly. "You're getting blood on the tablecloth. It's very hard to get blood stains out."

"A Band-Aid, I need a Band-Aid!" Mr. Whipple said, his voice muffled because his thumb was in his mouth.

"Not supposed to talk with your mouth full, Daddy," said Beatrice, who had stopped crying.

Alice giggled.

"Alice, go and get your father a Band-Aid. They're in the drawer next to the napkins." Mrs. Whipple served the slices of roast that had been carved before the mishap.

Alice went into the kitchen.

"No string beans for me," Beatrice announced.

"Just one or two," said her mother. "It's important to taste different kinds of food."

"But I already *know* I don't like them."

"Don't argue with your mother."

"Big or little?" called Alice from the kitchen.

"Big or little what?"

"Band-Aids."

"For heaven's sake," cried her father. "Hurry up! Bring the whole box."

Alice rushed back to the table with the box of Band-Aids. Her father quickly pulled out a few and started opening them.

"Oh, Daddy, just a second. I thought of something we could do right now before you put on the Band-Aid."

"What's that?" he asked suspiciously.

"I'll be right back." Alice pushed out her chair and dashed into her bedroom.

"I bet I know what she's going to do," said Beatrice smugly. "More science stuff."

Moments later, Alice returned. "Here, Daddy, just squeeze a drop of blood from your thumb on here. I'm going to make a blood slide for the microscope in Science class." Alice held out the strip of glass.

"Ah-h-h-h-h, yuck! Blood!" shrieked Beatrice.

"Oh, all right," said Mr. Whipple. "Here's a drop." He actually got so interested as Alice smeared his blood across the slide with the edge of another slide that he forgot about his thumb.

"Gerald! Your finger!" shouted Mrs. Whipple. "It's dripping."

Finally, Mr. Whipple got the Band-Aid on his thumb. Alice prepared her slide and Mrs. Whipple finished serving dinner.

"Boas make wonderful pets, Daddy," said Alice, getting back to her subject during dessert. "And they don't have any fur." She mentioned the fur because Beatrice had allergies, and the pediatrician advised the Whipples against pets with fur.

"But you have a goldfish and a chameleon already," Mr. Whipple pointed out. "You don't *need* another pet."

"Virginia Robinson has one," Alice persisted. "When it was a baby, she brought it into school for Show and Tell. But she's in the seventh grade. No one in fourth grade has a boa constrictor."

"Who's Virginia Robinson?"

"Mrs. Robinson's daughter," said Mrs. Whipple.

"And who is Mrs. Robinson?"

"Oh, Daddy, you never listen. She's my science teacher. Mommy *told* you we're studying reptiles this fall."

"That doesn't mean you have to *have* a reptile. Last year you studied Eskimos and we didn't get an Eskimo."

Beatrice giggled.

"But I didn't *want* an Eskimo. I want a boa constrictor. They're very interesting animals, you know. When they shed their skin, they turn a milky color and their eyes glaze over. It's called 'being in an opaque.' Mrs. Robinson told us *her* boa was shedding last week."

"You don't say. It all sounds quite educational." Mrs. Whipple liked to encourage the spirit of scientific inquiry in her children.

"Don't they teach you about Greeks and Romans at that school?" asked Mr. Whipple, who took a more classical view of life.

"Indians, Daddy. Oh, and did you know that boas are the most primitive snakes?"

"Really?"

"Yes, that means they don't have teeth."

"Neither do babies," observed Beatrice. "And Grandpa doesn't have teeth."

"How do they eat?" inquired Alice's mother.

"Well, Mrs. Robinson says they have a bony thing called 'cartilage.' It's like a fork in their throats. The fork sort of tears up the food as they swallow it. It's like peristalsis. But it's in their esophagus, not their intestine."

"Must we have an anatomy lesson at dinner?" Mr.

Whipple gulped his coffee. "A snake like that would poison us all in our beds."

"Don't be silly, Daddy. Boas have no poison. They don't bite. They're constrictors. That means they squeeze."

"I'd rather not be squeezed either, if it comes to that."

"But I'd keep him in his cage . . ."

"That's what you said about the rabbit. Remember the rabbit?"

Alice remembered the rabbit well. At Miss Barton's School, animals were considered an educational experience for city children. The kindergarten teacher was always eager to find weekend and vacation families for Robert, the class rabbit. If she didn't, then she had to take him home with her. Alice's mother had agreed to have Robert for a long weekend, because when Alice was in kindergarten, Beatrice was an infant. Her parents didn't know about her allergies yet.

So, early one Friday afternoon, Alice had come home with a big cage. It had a sign on top that said: ROBERT, MISS BARTON'S SCHOOL RABBIT. Alice had put the cage under the kitchen table and fed Robert lettuce, carrots, celery, and some special dried rabbit food.

"Do you remember how much that thing ate? Whole heads of lettuce in a couple of hours. Nearly ate us out of house and home."

"Rabbits don't eat houses," Beatrice interrupted.

"Oh shut up," said Alice. "Boa constrictors don't eat lettuce, Daddy."

"Oh? And what *do* boa constrictors eat?"

"Rats and mice."

"Rats and mice?" Mrs. Whipple gasped. "We can't have rats and mice around here. I pay a fortune to the exterminator as it is."

"*Dead* rats and mice," Alice added. "And actually Mrs. Robinson only gives mice to her boa."

Alice's father was still thinking about Robert. "He got out of his cage too. Shuffled around and woke us up before dawn on Sunday. And the droppings. Remember the droppings? All over the carpets. And the smell . . . and he peed all over my newspapers . . . and . . ."

"Boa constrictors don't smell," Alice said before her father could think of anything else. "Mrs. Robinson's dog has a very sensitive nose. He's a hunting dog. And even *he* can't smell anything. They're not wet either. And their droppings are neat, like white chalk and fur balls. You scoop them up with a spoon."

"Fur balls?"

"Yes. You see," explained Alice, "boas digest everything except the fur. So that's all that comes out. In little balls."

"So did Robert's," Mr. Whipple pointed out. "All over the place."

"And," Alice continued, "they only come out once every two weeks. It takes that long to digest a mouse or a rat."

"I wonder how much boas cost?" Mrs. Whipple wanted to know.

"Wel-l-l-l-l," said Alice, "Virginia Robinson's cost eighty-five dollars. But . . ."

8

"That settles it. It's out of the question."

"But, Daddy, I have an idea. Suppose I save up my allowance and buy it myself. Then can I have a boa constrictor?"

"It might take quite a long time to save that much," her mother remarked.

Alice's allowance was seventy-five cents a week. At that rate, her father figured, it would take at least one hundred and one weeks to save up enough money. The cage would be more.

Mr. Whipple felt considerably calmer once he realized how long it would take. Maybe by that time Alice would have forgotten about it. She would probably be up to another species in Science and have a new idea.

Alice, however, was not discouraged. In fact, she already knew that you could get boas for much less if they were not breeding stock. She would check with Mrs. Robinson at school and find out about the cheaper variety.

"Hooray! Then I *can* do it. Oh, thank you. Here," she said, "let me do the dishes tonight."

2
No More Candy

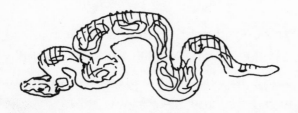

The next afternoon, when Alice and Beatrice got home from school, they played outside on the sidewalk for a while. Mrs. Whipple kept an eye on them from the kitchen window. One of the things she liked best about the apartment was that it was on the second floor and the kitchen window looked onto the street. That way Mrs. Whipple could fix dinner and watch Alice and Beatrice.

Sometimes the boys from down the block came over to join them.

Peter and James Hildreth were the same ages as Alice and Beatrice. Trouble was, Alice and Beatrice never knew when the boys were going to be nice and when they were going to be bullies. Boys were so unpredictable. Peter and James went to public school. They called

Alice and Beatrice "Miss Barton's Brats" and teased them about their school uniforms.

Alice was jumping up and down on her pogo stick. Beatrice had the job of counting the jumps, but she always went from eleven to fourteen so the count was never accurate.

Alice saw Peter and James race around the corner and head up the block. When the boys saw Alice and Beatrice on the sidewalk with Mrs. Whipple watching them, they knew they were safe. They slowed down to a walk and pretended nothing was wrong. Alice knew that Peter and James usually got chased home by a gang of older boys at their school. But they would never admit it.

"Hey there, brats!" called Peter.

"Hi, creeps," retorted Alice.

"Let's go buy some candy. I got my allowance today."

"Can't," said Alice. "You go."

"Can't?" Peter stopped and looked from Alice to Beatrice and back again.

"Saving up for a boa constrictor," replied Alice, still jumping.

Beatrice stopped counting. She and James didn't have allowances yet.

"Is she for real?" Peter asked Beatrice.

"What's a boa conspikker?" said James.

"Con-stric-tor," said Alice very slowly, hopping down from the pogo stick.

"It's a snake," Beatrice said. "A big snake that gets around your neck and squeezes you to death. It only squeezes boys."

"I have to buy it myself with my own money," explained Alice. "So I can't go squandering my allowance on silly things."

"Candy's not silly," said James.

"That's what *you* say."

"Come on, James," Peter said. "Let's go get our own candy."

Beatrice started to worry. She was used to sharing Alice's candy with her. Events seemed to be getting out of hand with the flurry over the boa constrictor. After all, it would be Alice's boa constrictor, so why should she, Beatrice, have to go without candy? She felt forgotten and left out. It wasn't fair.

Beatrice felt even worse when Peter and James returned with slurpy brown mustaches and their chocolate bars all gone. They had chocolate on their teeth too.

"Sugar's bad for you, you know," said Alice. "You'll get cavities and your teeth will fall out."

"Boa constrictors don't have teeth," Beatrice reminded Alice.

Peter wanted to have a turn on Alice's pogo stick but he didn't dare ask because he felt guilty about not sharing his chocolate.

"How much do you have to save for a boa constrictor?" he asked instead, wondering when Alice would be able to spend her allowance again.

"I know where they only cost twenty-five dollars. Mrs. Robinson told me about a pet store in Greenwich Village . . ."

Peter had heard enough. "Twenty-five dollars!" he

said so loudly that he startled Mrs. Miller, the nearsighted old lady from across the street. She happened to be walking by with Queen Anne's Lace, her white French poodle.

Peter thought that was a silly name for a dog. In fact, he thought the dog was silly, but she made a lot of growling noises and sounded sinister. He supposed she was a good watchdog, which is what little old ladies who live in New York City need. Peter wished he had a watchdog to protect him from that gang of older boys. Especially when they took his allowance on the way to the candy store.

"Oh! Hello, children," said Mrs. Miller, when she regained her composure and realized she was not being mugged for twenty-five dollars.

"Hello, Mrs. Miller." Peter's thoughts returned to the candy problem. "Do you realize," he said to Alice, "how long it's going to take you to save up twenty-five dollars?"

"Of course I do. I divided seventy-five cents into twenty-five dollars last night. It goes thirty-three point three three three three to infinity times."

"What's infinity?" asked James.

"Forever," replied Peter, looking glum.

James and Beatrice were worried.

"That's thirty-three and a third weeks!" Peter was appalled. "Thirty-four, after you round it up a week."

"How many seconds in thirty-four weeks?" Beatrice wanted to know.

"Millions and trillions," declared Peter. "What about a cage? Do you have to save up for that too?"

Alice had already considered the cage. "Of course I do. My boa constrictor has to have somewhere to sleep. They need a lot of heat because they are cold-blooded. It's called 'poikilothermous.' That means they have no body heat like we do and they take their warmth from the air. They like to be cozy. That's why snakes curl up under rocks or lie in the sun. You have to keep the cage at eighty-five degrees by putting an ultraviolet light bulb over it."

"How much is a cage?" Peter was looking at things purely from the financial angle, and it seemed to him that expenses were skyrocketing.

"Ten dollars," admitted Alice. "And you have to put grated corncobs at the bottom of the cage."

"At least corn is cheap," sighed Peter. "And I suppose you know that seventy-five cents goes into ten dollars thirteen point three three three three to infinity times?"

"Of course."

"We'll never have any more candy in our whole lives," wailed Beatrice.

"Don't be silly!" snapped Alice. "We'll just think of a way to make extra money." Alice hadn't actually thought about earning money before. Now that Peter had made such a fuss about it, Alice realized that she was in for a long wait.

"How?" Peter and James and Beatrice all looked at Alice.

"Girls can't make money," Peter declared.

"What *do* you mean? My mother makes money. She teaches."

"Your mother's not a girl. She's a grownup. That's different. You're just a girl who goes to a sissy school."

Alice was getting angry, but she knew that she was on the spot. "We'll have a toy sale. I'll collect all the toys I've outgrown and set up a stand on the corner."

"You can't do that," Beatrice whined. "I always get your old toys. I won't have anything to play with. I'll be an orphan. I'll starve. I'll . . ."

"Oh, shut up!"

Beatrice cried. She cried so hard that Mrs. Whipple could hear her up in the kitchen. She leaned out the window and asked what was going on.

"Nothing," said Alice. "She's being stupid."

Beatrice cried harder. "Alice is going to sell all our toys . . ."

"They're not *our* toys, they're *my* toys."

Peter and James just stood there. Their heads turned from Alice to Beatrice and back again, as if they were watching a Ping-Pong game.

"Maybe a lemonade stand?" suggested Peter.

"Bor-r-ring," said Alice. "Anyway it's too cold. Nobody buys lemonade in cold weather."

Mrs. Whipple called out. "Time to come in and do your homework and get ready for supper."

Saved by the bell, thought Alice. She was glad she didn't have to think of new ways to make money. She would lose face with Peter and James if they knew that she hadn't made a definite plan. Especially after she had bragged about it.

Later, just before climbing into bed, Alice added her allowance for that week to the few dollars she had already saved. She kept her money in an elephant-shaped piggy-bank. Beatrice was already asleep. "I'll show those boys how girls make money," Alice told herself with conviction.

3
Money Problems

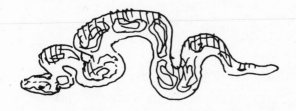

"And that's the story of Thomas Edison, inventor of the electric light bulb." Miss Renquist, Alice's Language Arts teacher, closed the book and adjusted her glasses. It was Friday and the fourth grade had spent the entire week reading Thomas Edison's biography. The theme for the fall quarter in Language Arts was inventions and inventors.

Alice raised her hand. "Did he make a lot of money on the light bulb?"

"Well, now" — Miss Renquist thought for a minute, a little startled by the question — "I'll have to check on that and let you know."

"That means she has no idea," whispered Sarah Jamison, who sat next to Alice. Sarah was Alice's best friend at Miss Barton's. They shared their most important secrets with each other. Sarah had a younger brother,

Timothy, who was as big a pest as Beatrice. Alice was sure that Sarah would be excited about the boa constrictor. Sarah had a dog *and* a cat. *Her* little brother didn't have allergies, so she wasn't stuck with fish and a chameleon the way Alice was. Alice could hardly wait until lunch break when she would tell Sarah her plans. Sarah would probably even be able to help think up ways to make money.

"Ladies, ladies." Miss Renquist tapped her desk. "May I have your attention, please." She peered sternly over the top of her glasses.

The girls' chatter died down and they looked up.

"All the Language Arts sections will now have an open discussion."

Language Arts meant reading. The class was divided into the A group, the B group, and the C group.

"Since each of you has read the biography of a famous inventor, we are going to talk about a few important inventions and inventors in history. We will start with the wheel." Miss Renquist looked around the room, which meant she was waiting for the girls to raise their hands. Several did.

Miss Renquist called on Lydia.

Alice and Sarah didn't like Lydia. She was the ringleader of the West Side car-pool clique, Hilary Jones, Caroline Williams, Elizabeth Ryan, Toni Carley, and Jennifer Stone. Lydia and her friends did everything together and they were snotty about letting others join them.

"The wheel is a very old invention," Lydia declared.

"No one knows exactly when it was invented, but it was an important step in civilization."

"Very good, Lydia."

Lydia smiled primly.

Alice didn't like the way Lydia bragged that she had the longest hair in the class. She wore socks with pompoms because she thought they made her legs look longer.

"Did the wheel make a lot of money?" Alice wanted to know.

"Why, I have no idea," said Miss Renquist. "What an unusual question. Since we don't know the inventor, we can't say. Certainly later inventions, machines for example, used wheels, and some of those made money."

"Oh." Alice thought about some of the things you could do with wheels, like make roller skates or bikes. But they were already invented.

"Does someone from the C group want to tell us about the telephone?"

Sarah volunteered. "Alexander Graham Bell invented it in Boston."

"Did he get rich?" Alice asked.

"I think so." Sarah hesitated. "But not at first. No one was interested in it for a long time."

Alice didn't want to wait a long time. It was already going to take a long time to save up twenty-five dollars for the boa constrictor and ten dollars for the cage. Thirty-seven point six six six six to infinity weeks as it was.

"And before that," added Lydia, who was also a know-it-all, "Samuel Morse built a telegraph. He used dots and dashes, the Morse Code, and sent messages. It took about six years before a lot of people used it."

Six years! Alice was horrified. Imagine waiting six years for something. Why, she would be *fifteen* years old in six years!

Then she thought of Louis Braille. She had read his biography during Library. He was a blind French boy who punched raised dots into paper so the blind could feel the words. That was a great invention too, but Louis Braille was poor his whole life. Alice was discouraged.

"Psssst!" Sarah whispered to Alice. "How come you keep asking about money?"

"I'll explain at lunch," Alice whispered back.

Hilary Jones raised her hand. Hilary was annoying the way she bounced up and down in her seat whenever she raised her hand. She wore jewelry to school and painted her nails. She and Lydia were best friends.

"Teacher's pet. Thinks she's so grown up," Alice said under her breath.

"The B group has been reading about the printing press," Miss Renquist continued. "Hilary, can you tell us about it?"

"Well," began Hilary, looking at her fingernails the way grownups do. "The printing press was invented by Gutenberg and he printed a Bible. That was how printed books got started."

"Yes," said Miss Renquist. "And the idea originated in China, which had developed printing by movable type about six hundred years earlier."

Wing Chu raised her hand. "Spaghetti is another Chinese invention," she pointed out. "Stirrups come from China too."

"Silly," said Hilary. "Stirrups are English. My father is English and the English invented horseback riding. All my riding clothes come from England."

Showoff, thought Alice. Thinks she's so great just because she has her own horse and goes riding every weekend.

"Yes," said Miss Renquist. "A lot of Chinese things were brought into Europe by explorers and travelers who sailed across the ocean to the Far East. Marco Polo was an Italian traveler. He brought Chinese noodles back to Italy with him and they became spaghetti."

"I bet he made a lot of money selling spaghetti to the Italians," said Alice.

Alice was excited when the lunch bell finally rang. The discussion on inventors hadn't solved her money problem at all. She and Sarah sat together at a corner table in the lunch room.

"What's going on, Alice?" Sarah asked eagerly.

Before Alice had a chance to answer, Hilary and Lydia passed by their table carrying trays. Caroline, Elizabeth, Toni, and Jennifer followed. They always ate lunch together at one of the big tables for six.

"Not there," said Hilary, looking straight at Alice and Sarah. "Peaches don't sit with Turnips."

"Snobs!" retorted Sarah.

Alice hated being called a Turnip. Hilary and Lydia

had divided up the fourth grade into Peaches and Turnips. They were Peaches. And so were all their friends. Everyone else, including Alice and Sarah, was a Turnip.

The Peaches had a secret code that they used when they passed notes to each other in class. Whenever a Peach had a birthday, the whole group would perform a blood-sister ritual in the bathroom during wash-up time. They had a password that changed every week and a hand signal that a Peach was allowed to use only when greeting another Peach. During Gym, the Peaches stayed together and were always on the same team. Alice hated being stuck with the Turnips.

Alice knew that the Peaches were snobby and that you weren't supposed to be that way. Nevertheless, in her heart of hearts, she wanted to be a Peach.

Still, today Alice had her mind on the boa and she was concentrating on making money.

She turned to Sarah. "I need to think of a way to earn thirty-five dollars quickly. Twenty-five for a boa constrictor and ten for a cage."

"A boa constrictor? Oh wow! What a great idea! You could bring it into Science class and let it squeeze Lydia and Hilary. Then we could take it to my house and strangle Timothy."

Alice had known Sarah would understand.

"Trouble is, I have to buy it myself. That means saving up my allowance. It's going to take forever." Alice told Sarah about Peter and James saying girls couldn't make money. Sarah was sympathetic.

"Maybe you could invent something," Sarah suggested.

"That's just it. Nobody seems to make any money on their inventions."

"Not that kind," said Sarah. "Something modern. Like the egg carton. The man who invented that made a fortune. Don't you watch the ads on TV? All those things make money."

Alice's parents didn't let her watch TV very often. Her mother always told her to read a book instead. Sometimes it was a big nuisance to have a mother who was a reading teacher. Sarah's father was in advertising. Something to do with ladies' make-up. Sarah got to watch TV whenever she wanted to.

"My father says if someone invents a new perfume or lipstick they get to be millionaires," Sarah continued. "Stuff for cleaning too. Like soap powder and floor polish. In fact, my father is writing an ad for a new cleaner right now. He brought some home and we tried it. It's going to be called 'Galaxy.' For washing dishes."

Alice was listening intently. She could feel the beginning of an idea inside her head.

"Hello, girls." Miss Renquist stopped by their table. "Is there anything bothering you, Alice?" she inquired.

"Oh, not really. No." Alice didn't want to tell Miss Renquist about her boa constrictor yet. It might be bad luck to talk about it before it happened.

"I don't want everyone to know about this yet," Alice explained to Sarah. "That snobby Hilary would be rude about the money. She has her own telephone and television in her bedroom. And Lydia has a Betamax. They never have to save up for anything."

"Cross my heart," said Sarah. "I won't tell. Not even Timothy."

"Good. Thanks."

When school was out, Alice and Beatrice boarded the school bus. Sarah lived nearby and walked home. "I have a plan for making money," Alice whispered to Beatrice. "But it has to be a surprise. Promise you won't tell if I tell you?"

"I promise."

"Floor polish. I'm going to invent a new super-duper-no-wax floor polish. To shine up wood. Then we'll sell it."

"Oh." Beatrice didn't sound excited.

"And you can help. *If* you do what I say."

Beatrice perked up. "You have to let me do something important."

"OK. You can be my lab assistant. All scientists have lab assistants."

Beatrice thought that sounded important.

As soon as they got off the bus, Alice and Beatrice ran down the block. Peter and James rounded the corner, also on the way home. They waved. But Alice and Beatrice were so eager to get in the house, they didn't notice.

"Boy," said Peter grumpily. "I wonder how long this is going to go on."

"Yeah," said James.

Mrs. Whipple opened the door and Alice and Beatrice dashed inside. Alice stopped short.

"Oh, no," she groaned, looking around the living room.

"What's the matter?" her mother asked.

"Oh nothing," Alice fibbed. "I forgot a book at school, that's all." Actually, however, Alice had suddenly realized that the apartment had wall-to-wall carpeting. There would be no place for her to experiment with her floor polish. She would have to think of something else.

Alice and Beatrice were having their afternoon snack in the dining room when Alice noticed the long wooden table. What a perfect surface for testing polish, she thought to herself. "I know," she said silently. "I'll invent a new super-duper-no-wax furniture polish! Tomorrow is Saturday. I'll do it tomorrow."

4
Alice's Invention

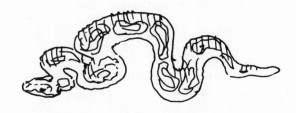

Alice woke up the next day to sheets of rain pouring down her bedroom window. A perfect day to stay indoors and invent something, she told herself. She had only to wait until her parents left for lunch and their Saturday matinee. Then she would have the whole day to work on her surprise.

"We don't need a baby sitter during the day," wailed Alice. "I'm in the fourth grade."

"Yeah," echoed Beatrice. "And I'm in kindergarten."

"Oh, yes you do," Mr. and Mrs. Whipple insisted. "We'll be out for several hours. Linda Lawson is coming over to sit."

"Who's she? We don't want a strange baby sitter. What about Margie? She was nice."

"Margie's studying for a test. Besides, she eats too much."

"She sticks bubble gum under the table, too," added Mr. Whipple. "Linda's not like that. She's the daughter of some old friends of ours who recently moved back to New York from California. You two be sure and be nice to her. It's been years since we've seen her."

"Yuck!"

"There's the bell now." Mrs. Whipple opened the door.

Linda Lawson was not what she had expected. Her hair was bleached a sort of silvery yellow and her face had so much make-up on it that it looked like a mask. She wore a purple blouse, blue jeans, and cowboy boots with gold embroidery on them.

"Oh, wow!" whispered Alice. "Maybe she's not so bad after all."

"Look at her fingernails," Beatrice said. "They're *green*."

"Come in, Linda dear." Mrs. Whipple decided she would make the best of things. She and Mr. Whipple were already late for lunch.

"Hi there, folks," Linda said. She entered, wobbling slightly on the high heels of her boots.

"What's that?" Mr. Whipple asked suspiciously, pointing to the large bag Linda carried. Clearly, it was not a pocketbook.

"Oh. That's my radio and headset. I never go anywhere without it." Linda opened her bag and took out a chrome box with all sorts of switches, buttons, and dials on it. The earphones were plugged in at the side.

Mr. Whipple was speechless. Mrs. Whipple said she

hoped Linda would keep tabs on the children and *listen* for any sign of trouble. "Come on, Gerald," she urged. "Let's go."

Alice and Beatrice were thrilled. No sooner had their parents left than they asked to try the headset. Linda showed them how it worked.

"I bet you could listen to music while you watch TV with those," said Alice. "The TV is in the study, through the dining room. There are three old movies on this afternoon. You weren't thinking of doing any home-work, were you?" Alice was worried that Linda might want peace and quiet like other grownups.

"Nah, no homework. You kids want some lime-flavored bubble gum?"

"Lime? Sure, thanks." Alice popped a piece in her mouth.

Beatrice was still trying to get the hang of blowing bubbles. Half the time the gum shot out of her mouth and stuck on something when she tried.

"Three movies, huh?" Linda's mind focused on TV again. "Who's in them?"

"Marilyn Monroe in the first, Douglas Fairbanks in the second, and Gary Cooper in the third. Channel thir-teen is having a movie marathon this month."

"Terrific. You kids got something to do or you want to watch the movies?"

"You go ahead," said Alice. "I'm working on a school project and Beatrice is helping me. Grownups aren't supposed to help."

Ordinarily, Alice did not tell lies, but she felt that this

was a special case. Inventors don't like to be disturbed when they're working on an invention. Besides, with a big stretch of the imagination, her new super-duper-no-wax furniture polish *could* have been a school project. After all, she'd gotten the idea from talking to Sarah at lunch and reading those books on inventions. She had even taken down the sign on her door that said BEATRICE KEEP OUT and replaced it with QUIET! PROFESSOR FIND-IT-OUT AT WORK! Alice's plan was to get Linda settled down in front of the TV so she could go back and forth from her room to the kitchen without being seen or heard. It was a good plan, providing the study door was partly closed.

"You could make a sandwich and eat lunch while you watch the movies," Alice pointed out. "The first one is about to start."

"Great idea. You know what? I think I like this job."

For the rest of the afternoon Alice worked on her invention. Once she was interrupted when Mrs. Whipple phoned. Alice assured her mother that everything was all right and that Linda was a terrific baby sitter. When she hung up, Alice tiptoed to the study and peeked in. Linda was blowing a very large green bubble. It popped and got all over her face and the earphones. Alice tiptoed back to her room.

Later on, the doorbell rang. It was Peter and James.

"Come on out and play," Peter said. "It stopped raining."

"Can't," replied Alice. "Busy."

"Inventing something," said Beatrice. She shut the door.

"Who wants to play with girls anyway?" asked Peter.

Alice gave Beatrice a lot to do so that she would feel important and not go complaining to Linda. Beatrice always ran whining to some grownup if things didn't go her way. Whenever Beatrice *did* start to object, like the time Alice told her to get the Comet, the olive oil, and the sponge from the kitchen, Alice reminded her that they were saving time. The sooner they made money from their invention, the sooner Alice would buy her boa constrictor and could spend her allowance on candy again.

Beatrice also brought the bucket her mother used for mopping the kitchen floor, and two large wooden spoons for stirring. Alice did the mixing. She began with a little water and added the Comet. That was for strength. Then, for smooth glossy texture, she added olive oil and a generous glob of her mother's hand lotion.

Beatrice did the stirring. Alice thought her sister looked like Mickey Mouse in *Fantasia* when he stirred the sorcerer's pot. Beatrice's arms were getting tired as the mixture got stiffer and stiffer.

Alice kept a careful record of the amounts of each ingredient, the way she had learned in Science class, so she could repeat the experiment. She wrote everything down on her pad of Paddington stationery.

When the bucket was about three-quarters full, Beatrice sat down on the floor. "That's it. Had enough," she declared. "Going to play with my Snoopy."

"Serious inventors don't give up so easily," said Alice.

"*You're* the inventor, not me. And it's *your* boa constrictor. I am going to have a rest." Beatrice took off Snoopy's cowboy suit.

Alice decided to ignore Beatrice. She studied the mixture carefully. Everything was smoothly dissolved. No lumps. Trouble was, the color. It looked sort of grayish-yellow.

"Snoopy wants a chocolate bar," Beatrice announced.

"Chocolate! Just what I need." Alice hurried to the

kitchen and took the can of chocolate syrup down from the shelf. She grabbed the can opener and returned to her room. She dumped the chocolate into the mixture and made a note on her Paddington pad.

Beatrice was interested again. "Can I lick out the bucket when you finish?"

"You can't eat this, stupid. You'll turn blue and die."

"Oh. Well, see if I care."

Alice could see that Beatrice was not going to be much more help. Good thing she was almost finished anyway. Now that her lab assistant was on a sit-down strike, Alice had to stir the mixture herself. At first there was a pattern of swirling brown and gray lines. It was like making a marble cake. Slowly, as the syrup blended in, the mixture became a rich, dark, chocolatey-looking brown.

"Perfect," announced Alice. "We'll get up early tomorrow morning and test it out."

"I want to test it now."

"No. We can't. It's almost time for Mommy and Daddy to come home. We'll have to hide the bucket in our closet until tomorrow as it is. Otherwise it won't be a surprise." Alice covered the bucket with Saran Wrap so the mixture would keep fresh overnight.

5
Disaster

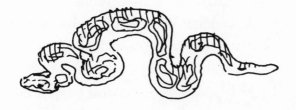

When Alice's alarm clock rang at 6:00 A.M. the next morning, she shut it off immediately so her parents wouldn't wake up. They liked to sleep late on Sundays. She decided to let Beatrice sleep too. Alice got dressed and took the bucket and sponge from their hiding place into the dining room. This would be the real test. The Saran Wrap had kept the mixture air tight so it was exactly as she had left it. A nice smooth creamy brown super-duper-no-wax furniture polish.

In the dining room, Alice put the bucket on some old newspaper to keep it from dripping on the carpet. She dipped the sponge into the mixture and carefully applied it to the table. At first it was difficult to get it even. She had to keep her strokes regular and they had to go the length of the table. Each time she lifted the sponge, there was a mark to show where she stopped and started.

By 7:00 A.M., the Whipples' dining room table was a rich, even brown with a slightly glossy finish. It looked brand-new. Alice was proud of her new product. You couldn't even see the scratches where Beatrice had scraped the points of her fork or the scissor dents from Alice's collages.

By 7:30 A.M., Alice had washed out the bucket, cleaned up the sponge, and scrubbed the two wooden spoons. It was still too early to wake anyone and the table needed time to dry. Alice went back to her room to read. Before she knew it, she was sound asleep.

At 9:00 A.M., Mr. Whipple staggered groggily to the front door and retrieved the Sunday paper from the doormat. He rubbed his eyes and glanced at the headlines. Mr. Whipple had the *New York Times* delivered every morning.

Mrs. Whipple made a pot of coffee, which she set down, along with two mugs, on the table.

Mr. Whipple handed his wife part of the paper. He kept the financial pages.

Mrs. Whipple tried to lift the coffeepot. It was stuck to the table. "What's this?" she said as she tugged at the pot. Finally, with both hands, she managed to pull it up. Something stringy and brown came up under it. Her mug stuck too. So did her hand. "Why, the whole table seems to be covered with dark brown taffy," she said.

Mr. Whipple wasn't paying attention. He was reading the week's review of stock and bond prices.

"Gerald!"

"Huh? What? Did you say something?"

"Gerald, your newspaper! Your sleeves!"

Mr. Whipple tried to look at his sleeves but they, too, were stuck. "What the . . ." The newspaper tore when he pulled at it, right down the middle of the New York Stock Exchange. That did it!

Suddenly a loud call jolted Alice awake. Beatrice merely grunted and rolled over.

"Alice! Come here at once!" Her father sounded angry indeed.

Alice glanced at her clock and saw that it was 9:30 A.M. Ordinarily Beatrice did not sleep so long, but she was extra tired from all the stirring.

Alice leaped up, shook Beatrice and half pulled her out of bed. "Coming!" she called back.

Beatrice was too sleepy to protest. She stumbled along holding Alice's hand.

Even before Alice got to the dining room, she sensed trouble.

"Alice, what on earth . . ." her mother began.

"Please, Mary. I'll handle this." Mr. Whipple's arms were brown all the way from his hands to his elbows. There were marks on the table too. His fingers were stuck together.

"Oh, no," groaned Alice. "You didn't wait until the polish got dry."

"Polish? What polish?"

"Oh Daddy, I spent all day yesterday inventing a new super-duper-no-wax furniture polish . . ."

"I helped," Beatrice pointed out.

"And you didn't let it dry," Alice finished.

"Furniture polish?" Alice's mother said. "What for?"
Alice hesitated.

"To make money," Beatrice answered promptly. "So

Alice could hurry up and get her boa constrictor and then we can buy candy again."

"So that's it!" roared her father.

"Please, Gerald." Mrs. Whipple turned to Alice. "How did you make it?"

"I made a list of ingredients the way we learned in Science. Let's see . . ."

After everything had been explained and the ingredients identified, Mr. and Mrs. Whipple decided that the most suitable action would be for Alice to clean up the table. Beatrice was ordered to help.

The mixture was not yet dry but it still took quite a while for Alice and Beatrice to get the table clean. If anything, Alice thought, cleaning up the polish was a whole lot more trouble than inventing it in the first place.

Later, Mr. Whipple decided to have a talk with Alice. He emphasized the virtues of hard work.

"But, Daddy, we worked very hard. All afternoon."

Mr. Whipple explained that it took most inventors a lifetime of study in order to come up with a new invention.

"But Sarah told me that a new product could make you rich."

"Very few people get rich that way," her father continued. "Look at the people with talent like artists and writers and musicians. They practice and study for *years* before they reap the fruits of their labors."

Alice took flute lessons and piano lessons so she knew about practicing. "Yes, Daddy," she agreed finally. "I promise not to try any more new inventions."

"That's a good girl," her father said. "We'll forget all about the table. You and Beatrice go and play for a while."

"Now what are you going to do, smarty?" Beatrice wanted to know if Alice had any more financial plans. Beatrice didn't see why *she* should have to help clean up the table. It wasn't *her* idea.

"Shhhh. I'm thinking. An idea is coming to me." Alice rolled her eyes, pretending to be in a trance.

Beatrice was impressed.

"I'm thinking about music," Alice intoned. "I see an old blind man playing the violin on the street corner with a tin cup in his hand."

"Yuck."

"I see another way to make money."

"You do? How?"

"It's a secret."

"I'll tell Daddy on you if you don't tell me. *And* you have to let me help."

"Wel-l-l, if you promise to behave. You'll have to wear a costume."

"A costume! Oh boy!" Beatrice danced around singing, "A costume, a costume. I get to wear a costume."

* * *

Next thing Beatrice knew, Alice was smudging soot on her cheeks. Alice made Beatrice put on her most ragged pair of dungarees, an old torn shirt, mismatched socks, and sneakers with holes in them.

"Hey!" protested Beatrice. "This isn't a costume. These are just old clothes."

"Take it easy. You look perfect. I still have to comb your hair and fix the sunglasses."

"Well, okay. As long as I can wear sunglasses. But it has to be the pair with clowns on the rim."

"Fine, fine," Alice said impatiently. "Now hold still or you'll ruin the effect."

Later that afternoon, Mrs. Whipple was in the checkout line at the local grocery store.

"Isn't it a shame about the Whipple girls?" she overheard a woman behind her say.

"Sad, very sad. Their father must have been fired," said another.

Mrs. Whipple hunched forward, hoping they wouldn't recognize her. She didn't dare turn around to see who was talking. She couldn't imagine what they were talking about either.

"I wonder how long they've been out there," the first woman said. "Right next to the entrance of the bank, too."

The clerk rang up Mrs. Whipple's groceries but she was no longer paying attention.

As soon as the clerk had bagged her groceries and put

them in her shopping cart, Mrs. Whipple rushed out of the store and headed straight for the bank.

At first, all she saw was the crowd. Then she heard the flute. The strains of "Good King Wenceslas," Alice's favorite song and the only one she knew how to play all the way through, limped through the air.

"Oh good heavens! Now what?" Mrs. Whipple pushed her way to the front. She was dumbfounded. "I don't believe it!"

Alice was playing her flute. Actually she rented the flute from Miss Barton's where she took lessons every Wednesday. The flute case was open on the sidewalk. Several people had put coins and even dollar bills in it. Beatrice stood beside the case. She wore sunglasses and the old torn clothes. Her hair and face were an absolute mess. Worst of all, around Beatrice's neck was a sign that said: PLEASE HELP MY BIG SISTER SUPPORT ME. THANK YOU.

Mrs. Whipple was furious. She grabbed Alice's flute, dumped the money on the sidewalk, and returned the flute to its case. Ignoring Alice's protests and gasps from the crowd, Mrs. Whipple took both children and marched them right home.

"But Mommy . . ."

"No buts, young lady. Just wait till your father hears about this." She was really mad.

"Hey, I can't see where I'm going," said Beatrice.

Mrs. Whipple yanked off her sunglasses and saw that the lenses were painted black. She kept them for evidence.

That evening, the Whipple family had a serious discussion. Mr. Whipple decided things had gotten out of hand. He would explain to Alice, and to Beatrice too for good measure, the realities of money. "Now, about this afternoon," he began.

"Yes, Daddy?"

"Really, Gerald," protested Mrs. Whipple, "what *will* people think?"

"Please, Mary. You see — " He looked at his children in his most bankerly way. His expression reminded Alice of the time he explained about where babies come from.

"You see," he repeated, "we do not *need* to beg. Begging is never a good thing anyway. It's better to work."

"But, Daddy. We *tried* to work on the furniture polish. And playing the flute *is* work. I practice three times a week."

"Yes, that's true. But you're not *ready* to perform yet. You've just started taking lessons. And furthermore, we're not poor. To pretend that we are is a fraud."

"What's fraud?" Beatrice wanted to know.

"Like lying," said her mother.

"Oh."

"If you want to be successful in business," Mr. Whipple continued, "you have to think of a way to manufacture a product that people will want to buy. And you have to be able to sell it for less than anyone else. Otherwise the customers won't buy it from you."

"I see," said Alice. "You mean undersell the competition."

"Exactly," declared Mr. Whipple. He turned to his wife.

"American History," Mrs. Whipple explained. "They are studying economics. Trying to make girls more aware of finance."

Mr. Whipple sighed. "Maybe we should send them to a boys' school," he said.

6
The Popcorn Plot

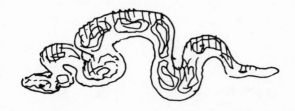

After another whole week of school went by, Alice
felt really discouraged. She still hadn't thought
of a good way to make money. And Hilary had called
her a Turnip at least *four* times.

"Tell you what," suggested Sarah. "Let's go to the
movies. They're playing *Wonder Woman*. We could go
this afternoon. My treat." Sarah offered to pay because
she knew Alice was saving all her money.

Alice got permission from her mother and went with
Sarah. Beatrice stayed home. Sarah's brother, Timothy,
was coming over to play with her.

"A whole dollar for a small popcorn!" Alice said,
standing in the ticket line. "And *two* dollars for the big
size. That's more than two weeks' allowance."

"I guess that's what Mr. Raines means by inflation."

Mr. Raines was the fourth grade American History teacher at Miss Barton's.

On Saturday, Mr. and Mrs. Whipple had been invited to lunch by the Whitneys, Mr. Whipple's boss and his wife. Linda Lawson was baby-sitting again. The Whipples couldn't get anyone else at the last minute and an invitation from the boss was important.

"No inventions today," Alice's father reminded her.

"No, Daddy, of course not."

When the Whipples had gone, however, Alice explained her new plan for making money to Linda. Linda thought it was a great idea and agreed to help.

Linda and Alice and Beatrice took all of Alice's savings. With her $1.50 allowance for the last two weeks, they added up to $7.76. They went to the grocery store and spent it all on popcorn.

About an hour later, they had popped and filled up forty-seven bags of popcorn. Each bag was sealed with a twist-tie.

Alice found Beatrice's old collapsible baby carriage in the storage closet and wheeled it into the kitchen. She filled it up with the bags. Then, with Linda carrying a folding bridge table and one chair, Alice and Beatrice pushed the baby carriage to the movie theater. They arrived half an hour before *Wonder Woman* started.

FRESH POPCORN: 75¢ A BAG said the sign in front of the table.

"Hey, look who's here!" It was Peter Hildreth. James was with him. They were on their way to the movie. "What are you girls doing today?"

"We are selling popcorn. It's one dollar in the movie theater for the small size. We're underselling them."

"Yeah," said Beatrice.

Linda was blowing green bubbles.

"Only seventy-five cents a bag, huh?" said Peter. "Okay, guess I'll take one."

"Only one?" said Alice. "What about him?" She looked at James.

"He can share mine," said Peter.

"Alice always buys me my *own* popcorn when we go to the movies together," Beatrice pointed out.

"I want my *own* popcorn," said James.

"Oh, okay. Give me another bag."

"Good thinking," said Alice. "You save fifty cents instead of twenty-five cents."

Beatrice was in charge of handing the bags of popcorn to the customers. Alice took care of the money.

The usher from the movie theater came over to complain. Alice thought his pointy nose and chin made him look like a weasel.

Linda told him it was a free country and he didn't own the sidewalk and who did he think he was anyway.

The usher slunk off. A crowd of children was gathered for the movie and he had a lot to do keeping them in line.

To Alice's delight, they were all buying *her* popcorn. *Wonder Woman* was a popular movie and it was not long before the carriage was empty. Alice had reached her goal at last. She had sold exactly $35.25 worth of pop-corn.

"How did you do it?" Mr. Whipple asked when he got home and Alice told him about the money.

"I just followed the simple capitalist principle of free market competition," she replied.

"I guess it's better than begging," said Mrs. Whipple.

"*Now* can we go and get my boa constrictor?" Alice wanted to know.

"Not now. It's getting late and the stores will be closing soon."

"By the way — " Something occurred to Alice's father.

"Yes, Daddy?"

"I thought you said Mrs. Robinson's boa cost eighty-five dollars?"

"It did. But then she told me about a new pet store in the Village where they only cost twenty-five dollars."

"I see." He knew he was beaten.

"Okay," said Mrs. Whipple. "Tomorrow is Sunday. Call up and see if it's open on Sundays. If it is, I'll go with you to get it."

"I want to come, too," Beatrice insisted.

Alice looked up the number for Species Unlimited in Greenwich Village. She called and found out that they were indeed open on Sundays.

* * *

49

It was quite a long bus ride down to the Village. But Alice didn't mind. She scrunched the $35.25 at the bottom of her Levi's pocket. She was proud to have earned it all by herself — with a little help from Beatrice and Linda Lawson.

Beatrice told everyone on the bus that they were on their way to buy a boa constrictor. Finally her mother read to her to keep her quiet.

Species Unlimited was not an everyday, ordinary pet store. It was more like a zoo. From the outside, it looked ordinary enough. All you could see were tropical plants in the window. Inside, it was steaming hot.

"Probably to keep the boa constrictors warm," Alice said.

"Hey, look at the blue fish with the long red tail," shouted Beatrice. "How do you tell if it's a boy or a girl?"

The animals were arranged in rows. There was a row of tropical fish, brightly colored and in unusual shapes, and a row of birds, all of which seemed to talk at the same time. Beatrice got into a long conversation with a myna bird. They exchanged insults for quite a while, until Beatrice noticed the monkey cages along the wall.

"Hey, look! The boy monkey is peeing!" Beatrice called out.

Her mother hid behind the fish tanks.

Alice was only interested in the reptiles. They were along the wall opposite the monkeys. She saw baby alligators, turtles, and lizards. At the far end, right near the counter, was the snake section. She quickly found the boa constrictor cage. Several snakes were curled up together. Each was a slightly different color.

"Over here, Mommy. I found the boa constrictors," Alice shouted above the noise.

There were a lot of people in the store, so Alice had to wait her turn. The young man behind the counter had long blond hair and an earring in his left ear. He wore a white T-shirt with a cobra on it.

"Is that a boy or a girl?" Beatrice asked, looking at the young man.

"Shhhh, quiet!" Her mother nudged her.

"But, Mommy . . ."

"Don't say another word until we get out of here," said Mrs. Whipple between clenched teeth.

A lady in a Chinese silk jacket was ahead of them. She wanted to buy food for her baby gorilla. A man with a ring in his nose bought three cockatoos. Finally it was Alice's turn.

The young man with the long blond hair smiled at them.

Mrs. Whipple nudged Beatrice again just in case she was thinking of saying something.

"I'd like to buy a boa constrictor," Alice declared. "A twenty-five-dollar one."

"Well, let's see," the man said and rubbed his chin. "I think we happen to have what you want." He went into the back room, separated from the front of the store by a curtain of beads, and returned with a boa in a glass cage. "This snake is not breeding stock," he explained. "That's why it only costs twenty-five dollars. Since it was born in captivity, it will eat dead rodents. I fed him today, so he won't have to eat again until next Saturday. He's a boy, by the way. The cage is ten dollars," he added.

"I have thirty-five dollars and twenty-five cents," said Alice.

"The bill comes to thirty-seven-eighty with the tax." Alice hadn't even thought about the tax.

"That's all right," her mother said. "I'll pay the tax." Mrs. Whipple didn't think she could stand another visit to Species Unlimited.

"Keep him nice and warm," advised the young man. "Eighty-five degrees is best. There is corncob in his cage. But you need a radiator or lamp over the cage."

"He doesn't look very big," Alice observed.

"That's because he's all curled up. If you stretch him out, he's five feet long. And he'll grow to ten feet. Here, I'll give you a little book on boa constrictors to take home."

"Thank you."

"Oh yes, one more thing," the man added. "You can't carry him home in the cage."

"What?" Mrs. Whipple was alarmed. "Why not?"

"It's too cold out. Wait here. I'll get you something." He brought out a pillowcase and a piece of rope.

"What on earth?" Mrs. Whipple began.

"Boas have to be kept warm," he said, taking it out of the cage and dropping it into the case. Then he tied the pillowcase opening with the rope.

"Can he breathe in there?"

"Oh yes. Very well. Snakes don't use a lot of oxygen. You'll have to put him inside your coat and button it up around him. The little girl can carry the cage. It's not heavy."

"Are you crazy?" Mrs. Whipple felt that things were getting out of hand. "I can't carry that thing around inside my coat!"

"But, Mommy," Alice protested. "I *told* you snakes don't *have* any body heat of their own. He has to borrow yours. Mrs. Robinson took her boa constrictor to the animal hospital inside her blouse during Christmas vacation."

"Bully for Mrs. Robinson."

Alice looked disappointed. The customers in line behind the Whipples were growing impatient.

Beatrice had her eyes on the monkeys again.

"Here," said Mrs. Whipple, "I'll carry the cage. In a box with a handle please," she told the young man. "*You* carry the boa," she told Alice.

The three of them, four counting the boa, who didn't have to pay the fare, boarded the uptown bus. They sat way in the back.

"It's warmer back here," said Mrs. Whipple, hoping no one she knew would be on the bus.

Snakes are lethargic by nature, especially if they are warm. But Alice's boa did squirm around a bit. She giggled that he was tickling her. The other people in the back of the bus were watching her.

"She's got a boa constrictor under her coat," announced Beatrice. "Doesn't she, Mommy?"

53

Mrs. Whipple looked out the window and pretended not to hear.

"That's very interesting, dear," said a little old lady with flowers on her hat in the next seat. "What's his name?"

"Sir Lancelot," said Alice who had just then decided what to call him.

"What a splendid name," said the old lady. "My son has a python. He called him Peter, which isn't terribly interesting."

"Peter python pecked a pick of peckled pippers," recited Beatrice.

"Pickled peppers, stupid," said Alice.

The old lady was still smiling when she got off the bus.

Once they were all safely home, Alice spent the rest of the day settling Sir Lancelot into his new environment. She put his cage on a board on top of the radiator in the study. Mr. Whipple found an ultraviolet lamp in the kitchen closet. He hooked it up above the cage.

Alice called up Peter and James Hildreth and invited them over to look at Sir Lancelot. They were impressed and asked all sorts of questions about him.

"Can he get out?" James wondered.

"He can," said Alice. "He's strong enough to push up the top of the cage. But boas don't usually bother to move unless they are hungry. They like to lounge around and rest."

54

"What a funny nose," said Peter, pointing to the little holes that look like nostrils.

"That's not a nose," said Alice. "Those are called 'heat pits.' They're for sensing the heat, not for breathing."

"Oh."

"This is boring," said Beatrice. "*He's* getting all the attention. Let's go play hide and seek."

"You go play," retorted Alice. "*I* am going to visit with Sir Lancelot for a while."

7
Show and Tell

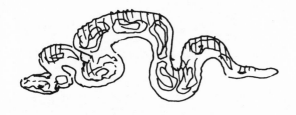

On Monday, Sarah came home with Alice after school to meet Sir Lancelot. They stopped on the way at a pet store to buy him a dead mouse. The store was having a sale on dead mice. Alice decided to get a whole bag full of them.

"You can't always get dead mice," Alice explained to Sarah. "So it's a good idea to stock up when they're available."

Sarah was really impressed that Alice knew so much about boas. Sarah was impressed with Sir Lancelot too. Alice let her examine his skin under her magnifying glass.

"He looks a bit like a pair of my mother's shoes," Sarah said.

"Yuck," said Beatrice, who couldn't understand what all the fuss was about. "All he does is sit around." But when Sir Lancelot's first chalky pellet and fur ball appeared in his cage, Beatrice perked up. "He doesn't pee like a monkey," she told anyone who would listen. "It comes out hard and white if it's number one and in a little fur ball if it's number two."

By Wednesday, everyone at Miss Barton's had heard about Sir Lancelot.

On Friday, Alice brought him in to Science class for Show and Tell. Beatrice helped her carry the cage onto the bus and into the Science room. Sarah arrived early to lend moral support and help Alice get things arranged. Science was first period.

"Wow! Look at all this stuff!" Beatrice said, staring wide-eyed at the animal pens, fish tanks, microscopes, scales, and other bits of scientific equipment. She shivered at the sight of the human skeleton dangling in the corner with labels on his bones. "Yucky."

The kindergarten didn't have Science and Beatrice couldn't read yet. "What are those?" she asked, pointing to some teeth in bottles of different colored liquids.

"That's an experiment to study what happens when you don't brush your teeth," explained Sarah. "The brown one is Coke. There's orange juice, tea, apple juice, and plain water. They all have sugar except the water. We're waiting to see which teeth will turn brown and dissolve."

"At least Sir Lancelot doesn't have to worry about that. He has no teeth," observed Beatrice.

"Oh gosh! I nearly forgot! It's time for class," said Alice as Mrs. Robinson entered the room. "You better get back to the kindergarten room. And thanks for helping me."

Beatrice scurried out as the fourth-graders began filing in to the Science room.

Friday was a half-day at Miss Barton's and the girls were allowed to wear regular clothes. Alice had been so absorbed in getting Sir Lancelot ready for school that she had put on her old blue uniform. Hilary, Alice noticed, was in her jodhpurs and riding boots. And Lydia was all dressed up. Her hair was braided and tied with red velvet ribbons. She wore party shoes. "My birthday lunch is right after school," Alice heard her say, even though you weren't supposed to talk about birthdays unless the whole class was going. Which it wasn't. Turnips were not invited.

"We are lucky to have a special treat for Show and Tell today," Mrs. Robinson announced when the girls had settled down. "Alice is going to tell us about her new pet . . ."

"Who cares about a silly old snake anyway," said Hilary, just softly enough so Mrs. Robinson couldn't hear. "England doesn't even *have* snakes."

"That's Ireland, stupid," Sarah retorted. "Good luck," Sarah whispered to Alice, knowing she was nervous about talking in front of the class.

And Hilary wasn't helping things.

"All right, Alice," said Mrs. Robinson, in the tone she used for announcements. "You may begin telling us about

59

your boa constrictor. Come up here to the front of the room so we can all hear you."

Alice felt self-conscious as she rose from her desk. Everyone was looking at her. Hilary made a face when Mrs. Robinson wasn't looking and Lydia giggled. The other four Peaches sat right behind them.

Alice made up her mind not to think about Peaches. She wouldn't even look at them. She looked at Sarah instead and immediately felt better. Alice marched up to the front of the room and stood a few feet from Mrs. Robinson's desk. When she turned to face the class, she realized that the girls really *were* interested in what she had to say. They were all quiet, waiting for her to begin. Only Lydia and Hilary were being difficult. Lydia was showing Hilary her nail polish.

Remembering her resolution, Alice looked at Sarah again, took a deep breath, and started talking. She was a bit shaky at first but she was soon carried away with her enthusiasm for Sir Lancelot.

". . . Boas move by contracting and expanding their muscles," she explained. "This makes them go in sort of an S-shaped line. It's a very slow movement, graceful, almost like a ripple in the water."

"How do they see?" Mrs. Robinson asked.

"Well, they don't see as well as we do. And they don't have eyelids so they can't close their eyes. That's why they stare at you." Alice saw Hilary blink her eyes and shiver.

"If they don't close their eyes, how do they sleep?" Wing Chu wanted to know.

"They make them into a slit to keep out the light."

"How do they know what's around to eat if they don't see well?" Sarah asked.

The more Alice talked, the more confident she became. Even Hilary and Lydia stopped bothering her. It occurred to Alice that Hilary might be just the littlest bit afraid of Sir Lancelot. Alice remembered how Hilary always refused to hold the class chameleon or touch the crayfish.

Lydia had stopped whispering and seemed to be actually listening to Alice.

". . . Those little holes on the top of his head, the heat pits," Alice went on. "They help him sense his prey. And the forked tongue isn't a tongue at all. It's the Jacobson's organ. It shoots out and picks up molecules sent out by other animals. The nerve endings inside the mouth read the information on the fork and the brain processes the information like a computer. Snakes do this faster than we see. It's been filmed by slow-motion cameras." Alice had done a lot of reading up on boas.

"How do they reproduce?" Hilary loved to ask questions to show how grown-up she was.

Alice was ready for her. "They have one opening at the back. It's called the cloaca. When the male entwines himself around the female, he fertilizes the eggs . . . Sir Lancelot is not breeding stock," she added.

"Not breeding stock?" said Hilary. "What about his pedigree?"

"He doesn't have one," Alice admitted reluctantly,

knowing how snotty Hilary was about the pedigree of her show horse.

"Alice has some slides of Sir Lancelot's fur balls," Sarah spoke up helpfully. "She made them herself."

Alice produced three slides and fitted them under the microscope lenses. "They digest everything but the fur of their prey . . ." she explained.

The girls took turns peering through the microscopes.

"Looks sort of prickly like a porcupine," observed Wing Chu.

"I had to separate the hairs to make the slides," Alice said. "Otherwise all you would see is a brown blob."

By the end of the Science period, nearly all the girls had had a turn at holding Sir Lancelot. Lydia giggled when he crawled around her neck, and said he felt like her mother's alligator purse only rougher.

Hilary was the only one who refused to hold him. She said she didn't want to muss up her new riding outfit.

Mrs. Robinson thanked Alice for bringing Sir Lancelot and for telling the class about him. She said Alice could leave him in the Science room and pick him up after school.

"Great job," Sarah congratulated Alice as they hurried from Science to Language Arts. "Everyone thought that was really interesting. I think a lot of the kids noticed what a scaredy-cat Hilary was."

"Thanks, you helped too."

Later on in the morning, when no one else was around, Lydia sidled up to Alice. "Hilary and I want to come over to your house and see Sir Lancelot again."

"You do?" Alice could hardly believe her ears.

Hilary strolled over, as if by chance, and heard them talking. Alice could tell that she didn't *really* want to see Sir Lancelot again. But Lydia had made such a big deal of it that Hilary probably supposed she would have to go along. "Well, just for a short visit," Hilary said. "Snakes aren't *that* interesting. It's not as though you can ride them."

"I *might* let you come," said Alice, pretending to think about it.

Lydia's face lit up. "I could show you how to make a tube sweater for him on my Knitting Nancy. I made a coat for my dog last year."

Alice knew all about Knitting Nancies. They had used them in third grade in Arts and Crafts. Still, she hadn't thought of making anything for Sir Lancelot and it *was* nice of Lydia to offer. Maybe she wasn't so bad after all.

Hilary looked bored by the whole conversation. "Bor-r-ring," said Hilary, studying the floor.

"Of course," said Alice, ignoring Hilary's remark, "I'd want to be a Peach first."

"Wel-l-l," Lydia hesitated. She looked at Hilary who looked at the ceiling.

"I don't know," said Lydia.

"He *is* a bit creepy," said Hilary.

"Maybe I could let you feed him."

"Really?" Lydia perked up again. She looked at Hilary.

"Oh all right. I suppose another Peach wouldn't hurt," Hilary said.

Lydia smiled.

"Of course, Sarah would have to be a Peach too," Alice added.

8
From Turnip to Peach

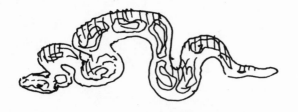

There was a lot more to becoming a Peach than Alice had imagined. In fact, it took a whole week. Hilary and Lydia explained to Alice and Sarah that they would have to perform a special task each day. And they had to keep it a secret.

On Monday morning, Hilary slipped a note to Alice in Assembly. It said: "At lunch today you must eat food that is all one color. Water is not allowed. You will receive further instructions later."

As soon as History was over, Alice and Sarah headed for the cafeteria. Hilary was waiting for them. "White," she whispered solemnly.

Alice and Sarah groaned. They felt even worse as they went down the lunch line choosing vanilla yogurt, cottage cheese, mashed potatoes, milk, and rice pudding.

"There isn't even any vanilla ice cream," Sarah moaned.

"It *would* be chocolate today," said Alice.

They sat together at a table for two. They wouldn't be able to eat with the Peaches until after their initiation ceremony.

"Hi, girls," said Miss Renquist, who noticed the odd assortment of food on Alice's and Sarah's trays. "Is anything wrong?"

"No. Of course not," gulped Alice between bites of cottage cheese.

Sarah smiled weakly.

On Tuesday, Lydia waited for them at the lunch line.

"Green," she whispered.

Alice and Sarah looked at each other. "Vegetables," wailed Alice. Sarah nodded. One at a time, they piled spinach, string beans, and peas onto their plates.

"At least there's pistachio ice cream," Sarah observed.

"I hate pistachio," said Alice. She reached for a bottle of ginger ale.

Lydia was right behind her. "No ginger ale," she said.

"But it's green," Alice insisted.

"That's just the color of the bottle."

"Well, it's yellow-green."

"Yellow-green doesn't count."

Alice was beginning to wonder if being a Peach was worth it.

* * *

On Wednesday Alice and Sarah had to wear one sneaker and one loafer and a green sock and a white sock. Green and white were the school colors. The math teacher noticed that Alice and Sarah had slight limps. She looked at their feet. "Your shoes!" she said, surprised.

"My sister hid the matching ones," Alice lied.

"So did my brother," said Sarah.

That afternoon, Hilary and Lydia gave them their tasks for Thursday.

The next morning, Alice and Sarah brought their book bags to Assembly. They sat in the very back and when everyone rose to sing, they snuck out. Alice went to the front hall reception lounge and Sarah headed for the Science room. By 9:00 A.M. both girls had joined the rest of the class for Homeroom.

"Did you do it?" Alice whispered to Sarah.

"Yes. Did you?"

"Yes."

Later that afternoon, the whole school was talking about what happened when Mrs. Partridge, the head-mistress, took prospective parents on a tour of the school.

"It was terribly embarrassing," Mrs. Partridge had been overheard saying to Mrs. Robinson. "Right there in the reception lounge. Someone put a red rubber nose and dark glasses on the statue of Miss Barton! What *will* the parents think of us?"

Everyone at Miss Barton's was familiar with the digni-fied marble statue of Cecily Barton, the school's wealthy founder.

Fortunately, by the time Mrs. Partridge's tour reached

the Science room, Mrs. Robinson had removed the school uniform from the skeleton. She decided not to mention it to the headmistress.

Friday was initiation day. At 10:58 A.M., six Peaches met in front of French class. "Synchronize your watches," Lydia announced. "You have your orders," she added, turning to Alice and Sarah.

Mme. de la Meuse gave a dictée. "Alors, mes enfants." She took a deep breath. "Écrivez: Le chat est entré dans la maison . . ."

At 11:07 A.M. exactly, three girls, all Peaches, raised both hands, the emergency signal for going to the bathroom. Mme. de la Meuse excused them.

At 11:09 A.M. exactly, three more Peaches raised both hands and were excused.

At 11:11 A.M. exactly, Alice's and Sarah's hands went up.

"Mais qu'est-ce que se passe?" asked Mme. de la Meuse. But she nodded, letting Alice and Sarah leave the room.

"We better hurry," Alice said. She and Sarah knocked three times on the bathroom door.

"Enter, O Peachlets," said the six Peaches in unison.

Alice opened the door. The bathroom was dark. The lights were off and the window shade was drawn. Slowly, Alice and Sarah entered.

Hilary stepped forward. "Are you ready to take the oath?"

"We are."

"Very well. Repeat after me."

Alice and Sarah repeated the oath: "We, the Peaches,

do hereby swear to uphold the principles of Peachdom.

"One. Never to reveal our weekly password to Turnips or sit with them on the bus.

"Two. To defend and protect the honor of each and every Peach.

"Three. Never to wear the school uniform on Fridays.

"Four. To carry the Peach insignia in our uniform pocket at all times."

"Welcome to Peachdom," said Lydia dramatically. She switched on the lights with a flourish.

Lydia handed Alice and Sarah a small cardboard coat of arms bearing three peaches on a field of green.

Alice and Sarah were officially welcomed into the Order of the Peach.

Suddenly, the firm footsteps of Mme. de la Meuse were heard coming down the hall. She flung open the bathroom door.

The ceremony came to an abrupt end as three Peaches dived into the cubicles. Three more turned on the faucets and began washing their hands. Alice and Sarah grabbed the paper towels.

9
Sir Lancelot Settles In

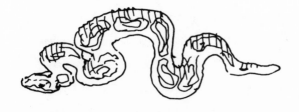

Now that Alice was a Peach, she felt better about school. In fact, the Peach password for this week was *Lancelot*. Lydia went to Alice's house several times to see him and invited Alice to her swimming party at the Colonial Club. Hilary asked Alice to the horse show at Madison Square Garden. The Peaches had a secret meeting and decided to dub Beatrice an honorary Peach.

Even though Alice knew that she owed her Peachdom to Sir Lancelot, she wished he were just the littlest bit cuddly, or furry, or playful, or noisy. She had to agree with Beatrice, though she wouldn't dream of telling her, that Sir Lancelot *did* sit around a lot. Not that Alice wasn't fond of Sir Lancelot. She was. She liked the way he crawled through her sleeves and wound himself around her arms. But she didn't feel the same passion as before.

In Science, Mrs. Robinson had stopped discussing reptiles. The class was now studying molds and one-celled animals. Alice was already growing penicillin on an old damp lemon and protozoa in a jar of grass water. In about a week, they would be ready and Alice could examine them under her microscope. The other Peaches were waiting eagerly for Alice to prepare a new set of slides. *Their* mothers didn't let them keep old food around and grow microbes in the closets.

Except for the fur balls and chalk pellets, Sir Lancelot was too big to look at under a microscope. He had to be studied with a magnifying glass, and Alice had already inspected every single inch of him. Besides, microscopes were more exciting than magnifying glasses. In fact, Alice had been thinking that she would really like to get a stronger microscope. Unfortunately, microscopes cost money. And Alice hadn't decided how to earn enough money to buy one yet.

One day in February, it was warm enough for Sir Lancelot to be taken outdoors. He would still need some extra body heat so Alice put him in the green and white tube sweater Lydia had made for him. She took him for a walk in Beatrice's old baby carriage.

Mrs. Miller was out with Queen Anne's Lace. When she saw Alice and Beatrice with the carriage, she thought the Whipples must have had a new baby. She peered into the carriage and, being nearsighted, put her head right under the hood. "What an odd-looking baby," she remarked. "Are you sure it's all right?"

"It's not a baby," said Beatrice. "And it makes fur balls instead of doo-doo."

"Oh."

"It's a boa constrictor," said Alice.

"Is it really?" said Mrs. Miller. "How very original. I'm sure it must be amusing."

Mrs. Miller didn't even scream. How dull, thought Alice.

Peter and James were roller-skating up and down the block. They were racing downhill as Alice and Beatrice pushed the carriage uphill. Peter crashed into the carriage.

"You idiot," yelled Alice. She was furious. "Sir Lancelot's in there."

"You're kidding. In a baby carriage? That's pretty dumb. If I had a boa constrictor, I wouldn't put him in a stupid baby carriage."

"Hey Peter!" said James breathlessly, catching up with his brother. He stopped himself on the carriage, giving Sir Lancelot another jolt. "Look who's coming!"

Peter turned around and saw three of the older boys from his school who chased them home.

"Uh oh," Peter muttered. For a moment he didn't know what to do. Mrs. Miller had gone inside her building, Mrs. Whipple was not looking out the window, and there wasn't a single grownup on the street.

Suddenly Peter had an idea. He grabbed the baby carriage and turned it around.

"Hey! What do you think you're doing?" Alice demanded.

"Shhhh," Peter whispered. "I'm just borrowing him for a second."

With that, Peter wheeled Sir Lancelot up the block right at the three boys. James followed.

"Let's get the sissy with the baby carriage," one of the older boys teased.

"It's not a baby carriage," Peter retorted. "There's a huge horrible poisonous snake in here."

"Yeah," said James. "It curls up and then jumps out and attacks."

"Yeah, sure. Very funny. Prove it."

Peter pushed down the hood of the carriage, leaving Sir Lancelot in full view. He was curled up just the way James said.

The older boys stared. They didn't say a word. Then they looked at each other and ran away.

After that, Peter and James began popping in to visit Sir Lancelot regularly. They even stopped calling Alice and Beatrice brats and teasing them about their school uniforms.

Alice let them look at the fur ball slides under her microscope. She also made a slide of a crumbled-up chalk pellet, but it wasn't prickly-looking like the fur balls, which Peter and James preferred anyway.

Ever since Sir Lancelot had rescued them from the bullies, Peter and James's interest in him had increased. They were even willing to clean out his cage, which gave

Alice more time to concentrate on her molds and protozoa. Peter would have loved to own Sir Lancelot himself, just to make sure the older boys didn't start chasing him again. He even thought about taking him to school and really showing those bullies. But he didn't think Alice would consider giving up Sir Lancelot and he couldn't imagine saving his allowance for so long.

Even Mr. Whipple was resigned to Sir Lancelot. It was not his most favorite animal in the whole world, but Alice noticed that he had stopped complaining about him.

Then, one Saturday, Mr. Whipple got very angry at Sir Lancelot again.

An important client of his bank was in New York on business. Mr. Whipple arranged an afternoon of golf with the client, a Mr. MacTaggart from Scotland. He had a bushy red beard and loved golf. Mrs. Whipple thought golf was a silly game, but if it was good for business she would put up with it. Alice and Beatrice liked Mr. MacTaggart's beard.

The Whipples had invited Mr. MacTaggart to brunch. Then he and Mr. Whipple left for the golf course, which was about an hour's drive from the city.

Peter and James came over to help change the corncobs in Sir Lancelot's cage. Trouble was, Sir Lancelot was not *in* his cage.

"Uh oh," said Alice.

"Hey, neat," said Peter. "He must have escaped. Let's hunt for him. We can pretend we're in the jungle and the cannibals are after us and tigers and lions and . . ."

"You and James search the bedroom," Alice ordered. At least there was some excitement again, she thought to herself. "I will be a tropical biologist and Beatrice will be my assistant. The two of you can be big game hunters and rescue me from the mad giant snake who is terrorizing the jungle."

Mrs. Whipple was putting away the brunch dishes. "I thought you were cleaning Sir Lancelot's cage," she said. "And, by the way, the lemon you left in the cupboard is getting very smelly."

Alice and Beatrice crawled past her, making jungle noises. "That's because the penicillin is growing." Alice explained about the lemon. "It'll be ready in two days."

"Shhhh," whispered Beatrice. "The cannibals will hear you."

Peter and James came running by with broomsticks, which they pretended were spears.

"There they are now," said Alice. She and Beatrice hid under the table.

Right in the middle of the jungle hunt, the apartment door burst open. Mr. Whipple stormed inside looking furious. He had his golf bag with him.

"Hello, Daddy," said Beatrice. "We're playing jungle. Watch out for the mad snake."

"Hi, dear," said Mrs. Whipple. "How come you're back so soon?"

Peter and James rushed past them, chanting and grunting.

"This is just about the last straw!" Mr. Whipple

shouted so loudly that the children stopped playing and stared at him.

"What's the matter, dear?" asked Mrs. Whipple.

"Matter? That snake is the matter. He's ruined my golf game. And MacTaggart went back to his hotel." Mr. Whipple was so mad he could barely speak.

Alice and Peter exchanged a glance.

"Where *is* Sir Lancelot?" Alice asked.

Peter thought it must be exciting to have a pet like Sir Lancelot. Something was always happening.

"*Your* snake . . ." Mr. Whipple began, looking right at Alice, "is in *my* golf bag. To be precise, he is wound so tightly around my golf clubs that I can hardly pull them out."

"But, Daddy," Alice said. "All you have to do is stick your arm in the bag and let him crawl up your sleeve. He'll be attracted to your body warmth."

"You don't say. Have you ever tried playing golf with a snake up your sleeve? Just as we were about to tee off," groaned Mr. Whipple. "MacTaggart was scared stiff. Wouldn't consider going on with the game. He hired a taxi to drive him back to the city. Said he wouldn't ride in the same car with a deadly animal."

"Sir Lancelot's not deadly, Daddy," Alice pointed out. She stuck her arm in the golf bag and Sir Lancelot crawled up her sleeve.

"Come on, Gerald," her mother said. "Let's have some coffee and forget all about it."

"Really, Mary," Mr. Whipple said desperately, "either that snake stays in his cage or he goes."

"Gosh!" said Peter when he, Alice, Beatrice, and James were settling Sir Lancelot back in his cage. "I sure would like Sir Lancelot for a pet."

"Me too," said James. "Hey look! Another fur ball."

"Maybe when we go away for spring vacation . . ." Alice began.

"Yes?" Peter's eyes grew wide.

"Oh no. You wouldn't want it."

"Want what?"

"It was just a thought."

"What kind of a thought?"

"Well, I thought that maybe I could *lend* Sir Lancelot to you. But you don't like him enough."

"I do too," said Peter firmly.

"He does too," echoed James.

"I'll think about it," said Alice.

10
Sir Lancelot
Becomes a Hero

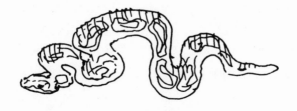

In March, the Whipples were discussing their plans for spring vacation.

"What about the animals?" said Mrs. Whipple, referring to the fish, the chameleon, and Sir Lancelot. "Who's going to take care of them?"

Alice had already considered the problem. Her solution would require some careful planning. Fortunately, shortly before the Whipples were due to leave, Sir Lancelot conducted himself in such a way that Alice's plan was sure to succeed.

It happened on a Friday night when the Whipples were asleep. Two burglars picked the lock on the back door to the apartment.

The Whipples were awakened by a sudden, loud crash.

"What was that?" Mr. Whipple turned on the light and leaped out of bed. His wife followed. Alice and Beatrice jumped up too.

Sounds of a scuffle came from the study. The Whipples rushed toward the noise in time to see one of the two burglars run screaming out the door.

The other burglar was on the study floor, struggling with Sir Lancelot who was wound around his neck. The TV was in pieces, scattered all over the room.

Alice marched right up to the burglar. "Lie absolutely still," she ordered. "If you move, my boa constrictor will choke you to death."

"Yeah," said Beatrice. "You'll turn purple and black and die."

The burglar did exactly as he was told.

Mrs. Whipple dialed 911 while Mr. Whipple stood guard over the burglar.

Soon they heard the police siren. Lights went on in the windows across the street.

The two big policemen who appeared at the door looked very reassuring indeed.

"Come in, officers." Mrs. Whipple held open the door.

"Over here," said Alice.

The police wrote down a lot of information and arrested the burglar.

Alice had to help unwind Sir Lancelot from the burglar's neck. He didn't say anything, but he went quietly with the officers.

"That's quite a snake you have there," they said to Mr. Whipple.

Alice smiled. "Aren't you glad I bought Sir Lancelot, Daddy?"

The next day, there was a story about Sir Lancelot in the newspaper. No one was sure how he happened to be wound around the burglar's neck. Alice thought he must have climbed up the door frame and then dropped down. In any case, Sir Lancelot was the neighborhood hero.

The phone rang continually. All the Peaches called to get the details. Peter and James came over for a firsthand account. Sarah and Timothy came too.

"I wish *we* had a boa constrictor," said Peter.

"I *might* agree to sell him to you," Alice said. "But only because we are going away. You'd have to take good care of him. He's famous now, you know."

"Would you really?" asked Peter. "Really, I mean? Of course we'd take good care of him."

"Wel-l-l . . . I suppose you have had *some* experience cleaning his cage."

"And *I* know all about his white chalk pellets and fur balls," said James.

"You'd have to keep the fish and the chameleon too," said Alice. "Sir Lancelot would be lonely without them."

"We have fish already," said Peter.

"You see. I knew you didn't really want Sir Lancelot. I guess I'll sell him to Lydia instead."

"I do too want him. Okay, I'll take the fish and the chameleon. But only for the vacation. I only want to *keep* Sir Lancelot."

"He'd be expensive," said Alice. "I've put a lot of effort into him. Lydia really wants him and she can afford to pay a lot."

"It's not as though he's a *new* snake," Peter pointed out. "He's sort of secondhand."

"But he's a hero. *And* he scared away those bullies who used to chase you home. He's mature too. He's grown several inches since I bought him. Suppose you pay me your allowance for the next fifteen weeks."

"Too long," declared Peter. "His cage isn't new either."

James and Beatrice watched the bargaining closely. Beatrice was thinking about all the candy she and Alice could buy with Peter's allowance. James was thinking about the chalk pellets and fur balls.

"Ten weeks," said Peter.

"Lydia offered twelve," said Alice.

"All right. It's a deal," agreed Peter. "Can I take him home *now*?"

"I guess so." Alice sounded doubtful. "Don't forget to keep him warm. I'll give you the ultraviolet light and his tube sweater for a bonus."

Alice helped Peter take Sir Lancelot and his cage up the block to his house. James carried the fishbowl and Beatrice carried the chameleon.

"What's all this?" asked Peter's mother as they trooped in.

"Sir Lancelot," said Peter. "I just bought him from Alice. He's a hero, you know."

Before long, Mrs. Whipple was on the phone talking to Peter's mother.

"Dead mice," she said. "Once a week . . . in the freezer . . . you'll get used to it."

Later that evening, Mr. Whipple was relaxing in front of the seven o'clock news. He noticed an odd smell in the study.

"Alice!" he called.

"Yes, Daddy." She peered in the door.

"Something smells in here. I thought you said boas don't smell."

"They don't. I'm growing molds. They have to be in a dark place so I put them under your chair. Be sure you don't move it around. They'll be ready soon and we can look at them under the microscope. Besides," she added quickly, "Sir Lancelot isn't here. I sold him to Peter."

"You what?"

"For twelve weeks' allowance," said Beatrice as she joined Alice.

"What on earth did you do that for?"

"Well," said Alice. "We *are* going on a trip. *And* I could save up some money from Peter's allowance."

"Money? What for?" Mr. Whipple was decidedly suspicious.

"Oh, Daddy, you'll never guess what we're going to be studying in Science after spring vacation . . ."

7